WARNE'S
WELCOME
BOOKS

THE JOKER OF DORMITORY D

WARNE'S WELCOME BOOKS

List of the Titles in this Series

BROWNIES AT ST. BRIDE'S.
BROWNIES ALL.
By Ethel Talbot.

DON-MARGERY SCHOOLGIRL.
TAM AT THE GABLES.
THE TWINS IN THE THIRD.
By Mary Gervaise.

RONA'S RIVAL.
BARBARA BLACK-SHEEP.
By Irene Mossop.

THE NINE O'CLOCK MAIL.
THE SCHOOLBOY AIRMEN.
By Alfred Edgar.

BOBBETY THE BROWNIE.
By May Wynne.

SHANDY OF THE SHELL.
By A. L. Haydon.

MYSTERY ISLAND.
By Ronald S. Lyons.

THE BULLY OF BOILING CREEK.
By T. C. Bridges.

THE JOKER OF DORMITORY D.
By T. H. Scott.

A TERRIFIC NERVE-RACKING BELLOW SOUNDED JUST BEHIND THEM.

The Joker of Dormitory D. *p. 61.*

THE JOKER OF DORMITORY D

BY

T. H. SCOTT

ILLUSTRATED BY

P. B. HICKLING

FREDERICK WARNE AND CO. LTD.

LONDON AND NEW YORK

Printed in Great Britain

CONTENTS

THE JOKER OF DORMITORY D

CHAPTER I

THE PROTEST MEETING

"WHAT makes it so funny is that it should be Billie. It's not like him. Now if it had been any of those Hill House kids, or a cad like Jenkins——"

"Oh, him! He wouldn't know a pound note if he saw one."

"But Billie," went on Jackson, too used to interruptions to pay any heed to them, "he always shares when he's got anything. You remember when he had those two half-crowns in one week—two uncles called——"

"Rather," said Bates, "and I must say he did us well there. Remember the tea at old Purcell's?"

"That's the time you made yourself such a hog over the jam tarts, Batesey?" asked a freckled youth usually known as Bozzy, his full name being Bozzielli.

"Hog yourself!" retorted Bates, who, being inclined to greediness, was always very sensitive to any remarks made about it. "Everyone knows you'd be standing with your mouth gaping open if anyone was throwing tuck about."

"Wouldn't be much that would miss you anyway," retorted Bozzy.

"Wouldn't it?" cried Bates, jumping up. "There's something that won't miss you if you give me any of your cheek."

"Shut up!" said Jackson. "If you want to scrap, go out and do it. This is a meeting, and we want a little quiet. We all know that Billie darling had a pound note on Monday—you saw it, Lucas, didn't you?—and so did I. This is Thursday, and he hasn't even asked a chap to have a bull's-eye! The question is—what has he done with it?"

"It's very strange," said Lucas. "Billie couldn't have a pound all that time and do nothing with it."

"D'you think he's lost it?" put in a mild-looking youth, Simpson—always called "Sim."

"Lost it!" said Bates, with great derision.

"Lost it and kept mum about it? Likely, isn't it?"

"Well, what has he done with it?" asked Simpson mildly.

"It's not what he's done with it," said Bozzy. "It's what are we going to do about it?"

"That's it," said Jackson. "That's the point. This meeting of Dormitory D is called to discuss what we are going to do with Billie's pound note."

"If he's got it," put in Simpson.

"Of course he's got it," said Jackson.

"D'you think we could get permish. to go to the Talkies?" said Bozzy. "Old Blinkers might let us." "Blinkers" was the usual corruption of Blenkinsop, the name of the reverend headmaster of Harleyford.

"And tea afterwards at old Purcell's—it'd run to it," said Bates.

"Not a bad idea," said Jackson. "Of course we shall have to find out first if it's the kind of film old Blinkers thinks decent."

"Where is old Billie darling?" asked Bates. "Anyone seen him?"

"He wasn't told of this meeting," said Jackson. "But it isn't like him to go off by himself.

He must be up to something, or he'd have routed us out by now."

"Anyone seen him since dinner?" asked Jackson.

"Yes, I saw him," said Bates; "he was just bolting out when I caught him—said he was going to the village."

"What did you say?" demanded Jackson.

"Say—er—nothing much!"

"Nothing!" cried Jackson. "You silly ass! Don't you see he may have been going off to spend the whole pound by himself?"

"He *couldn't* spend a whole pound in the village," said Bates. "No kid could eat a pound's worth."

"Eat!" said Jackson contemptuously. "Who said he wanted to *eat?* But didn't you ask him anything at all?"

"Er—yes, I did," said Bates. "Well, not exactly asked him, but I did say I wanted half-a-crown for—for a private reason and if he could lend it me——"

"What did he say?"

"He said he never carried such large coins about with him, as they stopped him running fast enough, and then bolted!"

"But he didn't go to the village," said Simpson.

"He did!" said Bates.

"Then he came back again pretty quick, because when I came up to this meeting I looked out of the landing window, and I saw Billie going up towards the Moor."

"The Moor!"

"He couldn't do much with a pound note on the Moor."

"He could lose it though—the careless young fool."

"Has anyone else tried to borrow from him this week?" asked Jackson.

"Well, I did show him an advertisement of a set of Iraq War issues for two bob," said Bozzy, "but he said they were a fraud, and advised me not to waste my money."

"I only asked him for a bob," said Lucas, with a sigh for his own moderation. "I owe it to that kid Blunden, and he can't forget it for a blessed five minutes."

"Did you get it?" asked Jackson.

Lucas shook his head.

"Billie swore he hadn't a coin on him."

"A pound note isn't a coin," said Jackson.

"No," said Lucas, "but I didn't think of

that then, and I thought perhaps I had been mistaken, and he hadn't got the note after all."

"He's got it," said Jackson. "I saw it. Now, look here—this has got to be done properly. This meeting of Dormitory D has been called to discuss what ought to be done about Billie's pound note. We must pass a resolution and put it down as a minute."

"A minute?" said Simpson.

"Yes. Here—you write it down, Sim, as I dictate it," said Jackson.

"All right," said Simpson, the meek, producing paper and pencil, "but don't make it a long one as I can't write much in a minute."

"Don't be an ass!" said Jackson. "Now—ready?"—and puckering up his brows in deep thought, he began to declaim: "'This Meeting of Dormitory D, held in Form III Common Room on this'—you can put in the date afterwards, Sim—'resolves that Billie darling'—No, don't put that, Sim—'Winthorpe Minor'—that's better—'that Winthorpe Minor——'"

"I say, the minute must be up by now," protested Simpson.

"You idiot!" cried Jackson angrily. "A minute isn't a minute."

"What is it then?" asked the puzzled Simpson.

"A minute's a—a——"

"A resolution," suggested Lucas.

"Same thing," said Jackson. "Now, got all that down? 'Resolves that Winthorpe Minor be told—er—told—er——'"

"He must share out," suggested Bates.

"No, no!" said Jackson. "This is a resolution. 'Resolves that Winthorpe Minor be told—er—told that—er——'"

"Whereas," suggested Lucas, who knew that this word usually figured in resolutions, proclamations, decrees, and all things of that kind.

"'That whereas,'" said Jackson, jumping at it, "'Dormitory D saw Winthorpe Minor take a pound note out of an envelope on Monday, and whereas——'"

"Half a minute," said Simpson. "I haven't got down the first whereas yet. I can't think if there's an 'e' in it or not."

"Of course there's an 'e'," cried Jackson.

"Two 'e's'," said Bozzy.

"And an 'h'," added Lucas.

"'H'?" said Simpson, startled. "Where's the 'h'?"

"You unspeakable ass!" cried the enraged chairman. "Put it where you like, but do stop blithering."

"Oh, all right!" said Simpson, and meekly went on writing.

"Now what have you got?" asked Jackson.

With much difficulty Simpson read out the embryo resolution:

"'. . . on Monday and whereas——'"

"'And whereas,'" resumed Jackson, "'—er—whereas——'"

"Where did you put the 'h'?" asked Lucas *sotto voce* of Simpson.

"I'll kill you, Lucas!" said the harassed chairman, and looked as though he were about to do so out of hand.

"Why don't you go on?" said Bozzy. "What's the use of all these whereases if you don't whereas anything?"

"'And whereas,'" resumed Jackson, after swallowing hard, "'the said Dormitory D are good pals of Winthorpe Minor, therefore Dormitory D calls on Winthorpe Minor to be sporting and share out.' Got that, Sim?"

Simpson looked up from his paper in despair and shook his head.

"I can't write as fast as that, Jackie," he said. "What comes after Winthorpe Minor?"

"Which Winthorpe Minor?" said Jackson savagely.

"Why, Billie darling," said Simpson.

The chairman was again on the verge of murder, but Bozzy created a diversion.

"'Be sporting and share out,'" he told Simpson hurriedly. "But what's the idea, Jackie? Suppose he says he won't share out or—what's the same thing—hasn't got anything to share. What do we do then?"

"I know," said Bates. "Let's bring him up here after prep. to-night and have a proper trial—just as if we were prefects."

"That's the idea," said Bozzy. "Jackie can be judge, and I'll be counsel, and the others can be the jury."

"But what's the charge?" asked Lucas.

"Having a pound note," said Bozzy.

"That's not a crime," objected Lucas.

"'Tis," said Bates, "if he doesn't spend it."

"But what's the sentence going to be?" asked Simpson.

"To stand treat of course at the Talkies," said the Judge.

"And tea," added Bates.

"But he isn't found guilty yet," objected Lucas.

"He soon can be," said the Judge. "Here, let's draw up a summons. Sim, you take it down."

Simpson groaned but took up his pencil again.

"'Winthorpe Minor is hereby summoned,'" dictated Jackson, whose father was a barrister, "'to attend in Form III Common Room to-night after prep., to—er—to be tried by his peers'"—murmurs of admiration greeted this masterpiece—"'to be tried by his peers,'" repeated Jackson proudly, "'for—for——'"

"'Unsporting conduct,'" suggested Lucas.

"'For misappropriation of public funds,'" said Jackson triumphantly.

"Here, I say," protested Simpson, whose objection, however, was only to the problem in orthography thus put upon him.

"When you've finished it," said Jackson, "I'll sign it, and you can deliver it to him during prep. Don't forget."

But at that moment a diversion was caused by the door suddenly being opened and a cheery voice asking:

"Hallo! What's up? What's the palaver?"

The new-comer stood on the threshold looking

at his assembled dormitory companions in astonishment. It was Winthorpe Minor, and it was easy to see why he had been nicknamed "Darling" —he was just exactly what a "mother's darling" might be expected to look like—chubby of face and figure, rosy-cheeked, blue-eyed, with curly golden hair, and that cherubic mould of features that *could* bear the most angelic expression but more often were lit up by a grin of triumphant mischief. For there was very little of the angel about Billie except his features, and they only looked angelic when he was asleep—or in trouble. Indeed, his masters were apt at times to regard him as more like an imp of darkness. His appearance now was greeted with an embarrassed silence.

"What's up?" said Billie again. "What on earth are you all up here for? Don't you know the tea-bell will go in half a minute?"

"We were talking about you, Billie," said Jackson affably. "Where have you been all the afternoon?"

"I've been out—looking for you," said Billie. "How was I to know you were all up here? What's happened?"

"But you went to the village," said Bates.

"And then you went on the Moor," said Simpson.

"Don't I tell you I was looking for some of you?" said Billie. "Fact is, I'm broke this week, and I wanted to borrow a bob if I could, just to——"

"Broke!" cried the company in chorus.

"Yes—stony," said Billie. "I've had no tuck since Tuesday——"

"But what about the pound note you had?" said Lucas.

"Pound?" said Billie. "Oh, yes—I remember—that was on Monday! I hadn't got any left on Tuesday. Hallo! There's the tea-bell. Jackie, will you lend me a bob?"

"I won't," said Jackson emphatically, as a rush set in towards the door. "And what's more, you'll hear more of this. Mark my words, Winthorpe Minor, you'll hear more of this."

"What do you mean?" said Billie truculently.

"I mean," said Jackson slowly and impressively, "I mean that you'll jolly well hear—more—of—this."

"What are you kids making all that row about?" asked Rodney, the prefect, coming down the corridor. "Don't you want any tea to-night? Cut!"

CHAPTER II

THE TRUANT

MR. ARMITAGE, who was in charge of the junior prep. room that evening, was considerably mystified by the behaviour of the little group of six Third-Formers upon whom he had learned by bitter experience he must keep a specially watchful eye. It was not that they showed any symptom of mischief—quite the contrary. All six seemed sunk in deep absorption. Now Mr. Armitage knew that such absorption could not be caused by the lesson books open in front of them—which were Latin *Principias*—and he was therefore profoundly suspicious. What mischief were the little beasts hatching? Instinctively his gaze went to the desk where he knew mischief was hatched as naturally as maggots in cheese, but Winthorpe Minor, seated there, was poring over his book, his features composed in their most truly angelic expression.

Nevertheless, Mr. Armitage's gaze returned frequently to this picture of innocence, and thus it was he saw Simpson surreptitiously edge a piece of paper on to Winthorpe's desk.

"Simpson!" he called instantly. "Bring that paper to me."

Simpson, white as a sheet, rose, picked up the paper which Billie apparently had not seen, and stumbled out to the master's desk.

Mr. Armitage took the paper, opened it, and read:

> "Winthorpe Miner is herby sumund to attend in form 3 comun room tonight after prep. tuer to be tried by his peres to be tried by his peres for for missapopashun of public funds.
>
> "Signed T. Jackson,
> "Chairman."

"This is in your handwriting, Simpson?" he asked.

"Yes, sir."

"You will be good enough to get on with your preparation and bring me one hundred lines to-night before roll-call."

He crushed the piece of paper into a ball and flung it into his wastepaper basket, then looked up quickly. Instantly, with almost machine-like precision, the fifty-odd pairs of eyes which had been watching him were fixed on their books, but not quickly enough to prevent Mr. Armitage from catching the baleful glare with which Jackson was favouring the unhappy Simpson.

"Jackson," said the master sharply, "close your book, and be good enough to conjugate *audio*."

Jackson, startled and at first relieved by the unexpected request, floundered through the first few words, but was soon hopelessly muddled and lost.

"It is as I thought," said Mr. Armitage coldly. "Instead of getting on with your preparation you have been letting your thoughts wander to all manner of nonsense. You will write out the conjugation of *audio* in full six times and bring it to me before roll-call."

"That's settled two of them," reflected the master. "All the same, I think I'll pay an accidental visit to Form Three Common Room to-night."

The rest of the prep. hour passed in frigid silence, but Jackson's seething anger was not the less for being suppressed.

"You silly owl!" he hissed in Simpson's ear as they made their way towards the Common Room.

"How could I help it?" said Simpson. "Billie wouldn't take it."

When they reached the Common Room they were quickly joined by Bates, Lucas, and Bozzy.

"Come on," said Bates. "You silly asses—we shall have to spurt a bit, or you won't get your impots. done by roll-call."

At Harleyford the prep. hour for the junior school was five-thirty to six-thirty and roll-call at eight-thirty.

"You kids will help a bit surely," said Jackson. "We're all in this."

"Rot!" said Bozzy. "It's your do. Besides, you've got plenty of time; you can get on with it while we're trying Billie. You're only the judge; you don't have to talk all the time."

"Come on," said Bates. "Let's get the room ready. How can we make a dock?"

"Why, put the table across so—Billie will stand there, wedged in the corner. I will sit in the chair at the top of the table. Bozzy will be counsel and Simpson clerk, and they can sit one on each side. Lucas and Batesey, you're the jury and sit over there. Bozzy, you ought to have a wig—a long——"

"But, don't you understand," said Simpson, "Billie won't be coming——"

"Won't he!" said Jackson.

"No, he didn't get the summons," said Simpson. "Mr. Armitage tore it up."

Now, although all five had been observers of this action, it had not occurred to them that Billie might not, in consequence, be favouring them with his company that evening.

"Then if he doesn't come, he'll jolly well be fetched," said Jackson. "Sim, you must be clerk and jailer; it's up to you to fetch the prisoner."

"I'll see if he'll come," said Simpson, and went somewhat dubiously from the room.

Meanwhile Jackson and Bozzy contrived to fashion rough imitations of wigs out of a quire of blotting-paper, and the Judge draped himself in a black tablecloth arranged as nearly as possible in the manner of a gown. Seated on the judicial bench, he made an imposing figure of stern justice. At intervals he rapped loudly on the table with a wooden ruler, and as the minutes passed and no prisoner appeared it was clear that the Judge's temper was fast rising.

"Usher!" he called.

"But we're the jury," objected Lucas.

"Usher!" thundered the Judge, with a resounding rap on the table.

But at that moment Simpson returned to report that he had searched all through the house and the prisoner was missing.

"Oh, oh! Absconded!" said Jackson.

"But where can he be?" asked Lucas.

"Looks as though he knew what was on," said Bozzy.

"What can he be up to?" ruminated Bates. "Did you look in the tuck shop?"

"Of course!" said Simpson. "And I asked young Blunden, and he said he saw him going across the quad. towards the nets. But I went to see, and he wasn't at the nets."

It was most astounding. Billie was the most sociable of chaps and the last fellow to go off by himself. Indeed, the Dormitory D six were regarded as practically inseparable, either in work, play, or mischief. The Judge was constrained to transform the two jurymen into extra jailers and send them off to search for the prisoner. But they met with no more success than Simpson, and both counsel and Judge had to disrobe and join in the search.

But it was all to no purpose. Billie darling was not in the house, or the school, or the playing fields. Bounds at Harleyford were pretty wide, and up to roll-call boys were allowed to go down into the village, a mile away in one direction, or out on to the Moor that stretched beyond the playing fields. This " Moor " was a piece of common land covered with gorse bushes and may trees and running to the foot of the hills, the slopes of which were covered with thick woods. The boys were allowed on the Moor, but the woods beyond and the cultivated land on either side were strictly out of bounds, and heavy punishment was always inflicted on any boy found breaking them.

When at last Jackson and Simpson had to abandon the search to make frantic efforts to get their impots. done by roll-call, the other three carried on. But all they could learn of the truant was that he had been seen going towards the playing fields.

The three searchers went to the Moor, but here their efforts were somewhat impeded by Lucas finding a toad. By the time it had been thoroughly examined, careful measurements taken of its leaps, and a fierce argument settled as to whether a toad did or did not have a jewel in its head, and if so where was it, and what it would be worth if sold—by this time roll-call was only a few minutes off, and all three had to rush back to school.

Roll was taken in the hall of each house by the head boy, and failure to answer always meant a visit to the house master. Bates and Bozzy were unfortunate in that the roll was always taken alphabetically, and B came most inconveniently early in the list. However, they just managed it, shouting " Here " almost as they crossed the threshold. Lucas was in plenty of time, but Jackson, who had had to visit Mr. Armitage first, had to answer before he had crossed the threshold, and was given " late " by the prefect at the door.

Simpson and Winthorpe, of course, had much better chances. Simpson, who had been detained by Mr. Armitage with a complaint of the untidiness of his lines, just managed his call, and then the five chums of Dormitory D looked eagerly round for their missing comrade. He was absent!

"Smith, Taylor, Watts, West, White," went on the head boy, "Win—"

There was a noise at the door—a scuffle of feet, and the sound of a gasping breath.

"—thorpe Minor!"

"Here!"

He was there right enough, but what had happened to him? His chums gazed at him in amazement. His face was crimson, his eyes were strained, and his breath was coming in violent gasps—as if he had just finished a desperately fought five-mile race. His hair was wildly wind-tossed, and—most amazing of all—his boots, clothes, hands, and various other parts of his anatomy were caked in mud. Mud—when there had been no rain for weeks and the playing fields and Moor were bone dry!

"What on earth have you been up to, Winthorpe Minor?" asked the prefect, as roll came to an end. "Where have you been?"

"On the Moor," gasped Billie. "I didn't know it was so late, and had to sprint for it. In my hurry I fell into a ditch."

"You filthy young beast!" said the prefect. "You go straight up and get those muddy things off and give them to Matron. She'll know what to say about *them*. But look here, all you kids—the proper time to be here for roll is *before* it begins—not just as your name's called. Mind that! Another time anyone dashing in like this will be late."

A minute later Billie was in the hands of his chums.

"Where have you been?" demanded Jackson, seizing one arm.

"What's the game, Billie?" asked Bates, seizing the other.

Bozzy and Lucas also had their questions to put, and Simpson hovered near.

"Let go!" said Billie. "You heard what Halford said. I've got to go to Matron."

"Tell us first where you've been!" demanded Jackson.

"On the Moor," said Billie, and wrenched one arm free.

"What for?" asked Bates.

Billie looked at them for a moment before replying.

"What for? I don't see it matters to you,

Batesey, but I'll tell you if you'll let go my arm."

Billie's tone was so sweetly reasonable that Bates let go.

"I went on to the Moor to see if I could catch a butterfly or moth."

"What for?" said Bates again.

"You were all so jolly mean when I asked you to lend me a bob, and I knew Blunt Major often gives a bob for any old moth if he hasn't got it in his collection, so I thought I'd have a try for one. You know, it's jolly rotten not having a penny for tuck for three days, and one's chums so mean—I'll see you in the dorm. later"—and Billie, with a deeply injured air, turned off towards Matron's room.

Nine o'clock was lights out for the junior dormitories at Harleyford, and all the lower school went straight to their sleeping quarters from roll-call.

It was two minutes to nine when at last Billie entered Dormitory D where the other five inmates, already in bed, were eagerly awaiting him. A very wholesome respect was felt for Matron, and it had been agreed that Billie was in for it now. But when he entered, his expression was almost seraphic. He was in clean pyjamas, his hair was beautifully brushed, and his whole being exuded that delightful air of cleanliness which one feels after a comforting hot bath.

"What did Matron say?" whispered Bates.

"Made me have a hot bath," said Billie, "and she's going to bring me a hot supper in bed."

"I should say so!" scoffed Bates.

"You'll see in a minute," said Billy, as he got into bed.

And, sure enough, a minute later Matron bustled in with a basin of steaming bread and milk.

"Here you are, Winthorpe," she said. "How do you feel now? Does your head ache?"

"Not much, Matron."

"Are the bruises sore?"

"Only a little, Matron."

"Well, eat that up and get to sleep, and you won't be any the worse in the morning."

While Billie was eating, Matron occupied her time by making a tour of the dormitory.

"Jackson, what are your clothes left on the floor for? You untidy scamp! Get up at once and put them in your locker. Lucas, you know your boots must not be kept under your bed. Put them away at once. Bozzielli, your face is very dirty! Show me your hands. Did you wash before you got into bed? You come to me every night for a week *after* you have washed. Bates——"

By the time Billie had finished his bread and milk, and Matron had finished her inspection, and had collected Billie's empty basin, and turned lights out, five of the inmates of Dormitory D lay glaring angrily in the darkness.

The sixth inmate, however, snuggled down comfortably into his bed, and with a deep sigh of content murmured as if to himself:

"That was jolly fine!"

Billie had "got away with it" once again.

CHAPTER III

A WEEK OF MYSTERY

THE week that followed was one of profound mystery and unending excitement for Dormitory D. They knew Billie was engaged in some daring escapade which, for some reason, he was keeping entirely to himself. He was frequently missing. No one knew where or how he spent these absences, and yet when questioned after them, he was always able to give a perfectly reasonable explanation.

It was so perfectly reasonable that no one could contradict him; yet five minutes later everyone was telling himself it couldn't be true. What was his game? Why was he making a secret of it? In some way it must be connected with that pound note.

Singly and together the "Dormie D's" made efforts to track their truant chum, but always he evaded them, and their vigilance only brought them a perfect flood of impots.

The Friday following the day on which Billie had evaded his "trial" had started sensationally, for when the "Dormie D's" had been roused by the rising-bell and had gained sufficient wakeful sense to be aware of their surroundings, they found that Billie was missing. He had got up and gone out before even the first bell had gone—a thing that had never been known to happen before in the history of Harleyford.

The "Dormie D's" were so amazed that they could think of no action they could take before breakfast, and when they assembled for that meal, still lost in wonder, Billie joined them—very red and hot and with a nasty bruise on his right cheek, which certainly had not been there last night.

"Where've you been?" whispered Bates, as they entered the dining-room.

"On the Moor," said Billie. "I went to have another try for a moth for old Blunt, but it was no good—moths don't seem to get up early."

"Where've you been?" demanded Jackson, as Billie sat down beside him.

"Oh, rats to you!" said Billie.

"What've you been up to, Billie?" asked Bozzy, leaning across the table to whisper—

"noise" was not allowed at meal times, and any attempt at "ordinary" conversation usually brought down a decree of silence.

Billie looked him straight in the eyes. Next to him was Lucas, also listening, and Simpson was a little lower down.

"Haven't you chaps ever heard," he said sweetly, "that it's jolly bad for the liver to lie fugging in bed when the sun's shining?"

Four of the "Dormie D's" tried to reply to this question at once, with the inevitable result—a stern command for silence from the master at the top of the table.

As the morning progressed wonder was added to wonder. All through the class hours Billie was a most attentive and industrious pupil, and Mr. Armitage was so puzzled that he had serious thoughts of reporting him to Matron as a suspicious case for the Sanatorium. His example, however, only brought disaster to his fellow "Dormie D's," who were so lost in astonishment at this change that three of them had been given detention before the morning was over.

This only left Lucas and Simpson to watch him, and these he easily escaped by suggesting a game of "I spy" on the Moor, and then hiding so successfully that they saw no more of him till roll-call.

The next day, Saturday, a cricket match was fixed for the afternoon between the Second Elevens of High House and Hill House, and four of the "Dormie D's" were leading lights in the High House team. Now High House and Hill House, being very close neighbours, lived in a state of the fiercest rivalry. Even a cricket match between them became almost as serious as a life and death struggle, and therefore on this day even Billie's vagaries were likely to be forgotten.

To the astonishment of the "Dormie D's," however, he cut even this. When Salter, the captain, put up the team, Billie's name was not in it.

"But—but why aren't you playing Winthorpe Minor?" demanded Jackson.

"Crocked," said Salter. "He showed me his leg—smothered in bruises—fell in a ditch or something. Didn't you know?"

"He—he did say something about it," stammered Jackson.

And that evening Billie did come back across the Moor with a butterfly net—Simpson saw him—and one poor specimen of a moth which, when offered to Blunt, was rejected with derision.

"I wouldn't give you a shilling for a million of those," Blunt told him.

Simpson, who was not a cricketer, and therefore had escaped the prevailing excitement, had accompanied Billie to Blunt.

"Hard luck," he said, as they came away. "But if you really want a bob, I could let you have it for a day or two."

"Will you, Sim?" said Billie.

"Yes. But we thought you were rotting. You did have a pound note on Monday, didn't you?"

Billie gave him a sidelong look.

"Yes, Sim, but I spent that on—on something special. I'd tell you, Simmy, all about it, but you couldn't keep your mouth shut—Jackie would have it out of you in a second. And it's a secret—by gum, it *is*."

"Is it something you're hiding?"

"Rather!" said Billie. "And you wouldn't think it could be done. I'll tell you soon and let you see some of the fun."

Sim looked a little dubious; he was of a law-abiding nature.

"But I won't have that bob, Sim, all the same. You see—I must go moth-hunting, or I couldn't keep it up."

On Sunday the matter was taken out of the hands of the "Dormie D's" as Billie was given an exeat for the day to accompany his brother, Winthorpe Major, captain of the school, and so far removed from the sphere in which the "Dormie D's" moved that the brothers only met on the occasion of these exeats—granted to them to visit an aunt in a neighbouring seaside town. But before he went Billie sought out Lucas.

"Do something for me, Lukey?" he asked.

Lucas looked at him suspiciously.

"I don't know," he said. "What's the idea?"

"It's like this, Lukey," said Billie earnestly. "There's something I must do—it's a secret, but I'll let you all in soon. I know you think it funny and all that—but there's something that must be done—something secret—and I'm the only one who can do it."

"What—what do you mean?" said the astounded Lucas.

"It's just this," went on Billie. "When I

come back with my brother to-night I've got to cut off sharp——"

"Cut off where?" said Lucas.

"Well, that's the secret," said Billie. "I'll tell *you*—soon. But if I don't get back for roll, be a sport and answer for me, will you?"

Lucas looked dubious. It was a thing he had done before, but it was always risky. Anyway, it was a kind of service that ought to be paid for in some way.

"I don't know," he said. "You had a pound note——"

"I'll let you in on that, Lukey, truly I will," said Billie. "If I was to get caught to-night and 'gated,' it would cause awful suffering."

"Whom to?"

"To poor dumb animals," said Billie earnestly. "Come, Lukey, be a chum, and you shall be the first to come in and share what I spent the pound note on."

"All right," said Lucas, although somewhat reluctantly. "Done!"

And he did have to answer roll-call for Billie, and, what was worse, explain to the chums after why he had done it.

"'Dumb animals? Suffering'? What can

he little blighter be up to?" asked Jackson the ıext day when once again the "Dormie D's" vere discussing the mystery of their chum.

"Don't know," said Bates.

"If he's got any fun what's he want to keep t to himself for?" asked Bozzy.

"Jolly unsporting, I call it," said Jackson. ' It's got to be stopped. I vote we track him to-night if he tries to cut off again. None of you got detention to-night, have you? Then what about following him after prep.?"

"But he's such an artful bounder—he just slips off. That may be all bunkum about going on the Moor."

"There's five of us," said Jackson, "and if that's not enough, we can have a whole crowd out to-morrow. Are you all game?"

They were, and Jackson laid his plans with a cleverness that seemed to predict future military greatness. Immediately after prep. all five were to slip out and take up the strategic positions allotted to them. Simpson was given the road leading to the village, Lucas the gate of the quad. leading to the playing fields, Bozzy the door of the house giving on the lane leading to the Moor, and Bates was to watch the private gate leading from the master's garden to the playing fields. Jackson himself was to take up a position on the roof of a potting shed from which he could see all the sentries, except Simpson, who, however, was in sight of Lucas.

They were all to adopt easy, nonchalant attitudes and not give Billie any idea that he was being watched, but the minute one of them sighted him he was to signal to Jackson by waving a white handkerchief round his head and then keep the quarry in sight. Jackson would then repeat the signal, and the other sentries were all to follow him.

Prep. passed uneventfully, all six "Dormie D's" managing to escape Mr. Armitage's unwelcome attentions, and at six-thirty the five conspirators bolted with the crowd across to High House to put away their books, and then take up their posts. Billie, as usual, evaded them in this rush to liberty.

Bozzy, however, had not been at his post for more than a minute or two before Billie appeared.

"Hallo, Bozzy!" he said. "What are you doing?"

"Oh, nothing!" said Bozzy. "What are you?"

"Looking for Jackie," said Billie. "Do you know where he is?"

"Rotting round somewhere," said Bozzy. "I saw you all dash off after prep. I thought you'd got some jape on."

"Oh?" said Bozzy. "And what's your little game?"

"Oh, all right!" said Billie, in an injured tone. "Keep your secrets. If you don't want me, I can amuse myself. Ta, ta!" He started to run down the lane, and Bozzy pulled out his handkerchief. But Billie turned to shout: "If you see Jackie, tell him I'm on the Moor!"

Bozzy gasped, and Billie had covered quite fifty yards before Bozzy had recovered sufficiently from his amazement to give the signal. He then started to follow Billie down the lane, but by the time Jackie had collected his sentries and got them all on the track, Billie was well away among the gorse bushes on the Moor, and Bozzy was still waiting at the end of the lane.

"Where is he?" gasped Jackson as he raced up.

"I've lost him in the bushes," whispered Bozzy. "He slipped through here somewhere."

"You priceless idiot!" cried Jackson.

"Idiot yourself!" said Bozzy.

"He's done us again," said Bates.

But Jackson was a born leader and an expert tracker. He knew Billie couldn't go far through gorse bushes and must come out on one of the paths. He made his scouts each take a track. They were to follow it up to the further edge of the Moor where the woods began and as soon as they sighted the quarry signal to the others by an owl's hoot. If they didn't sight him they were all to meet at the Dead Oak—a spectral tree known to them all.

Keeping low and running as silently as they could, they had progressed for about five minutes when Jackie was startled by a loud "Tu-whit" on his right. The next second he saw the quarry himself, running along a track that crossed his own path.

He turned along the track Billie had been following, and quickly ran into Lucas and Bates. Bozzy joined them and then Simpson, and all settled down to a steady run. But no further sight of the quarry was vouchsafed to them, and they all pulled up as the path ended at a high gate set in the thick-set hedge which separated the Moor from the woods, and represented their bounds. Beyond this they dared not go.

"Where's he got to?" whispered Jackson.

But no one could answer. They had all seen him running along this track. He wouldn't dare go out of bounds. He must therefore be hiding somewhere on the Moor. They had just turned to retrace their steps and search for traces of him, when a loud "Tu-whit!" rang out from the woods.

Now although this had been their agreed signal and they had had no doubt at all that, if Billie heard it, he would only think it was an early owl, they none of them for a moment doubted that the cry they had just heard was not from an owl but a human imitator. Who could have done it? Why, Billie of course.

They crowded to the gate and peered through the railings. The gate gave on a long glade running through the thick growth of the wood, and in the dim, twilit distance they saw a form —a boy running. He stopped and turned for a moment.

"Tu-whit!" came echoing down the glade, and then he vanished amid the trees.

There was an awed silence among the watchers.

"It was him," said Bozzy at last.

"Out of bounds!" breathed Simpson.

"That's where the mud comes from," said Bates.

"But why?" asked Lucas.

"That's it. Why?" said Jackson. "We've got to find out."

"We—we can't go out of bounds," said Simpson.

"It would mean going to Blinkers if we were caught," said Bozzy.

"Billie's done it," said Jackson. "He doesn't funk it."

"I'll tell you what," said Bates. "He's got to come back. You're not answering roll for him to-night, Lukey, are you?"

"No," said Lucas.

"Then why not stay here and get him as he comes back?"

"What good'll that do?" asked Jackson. "That won't tell us where he's been."

"We can seize him and threaten to take him to his brother for breaking bounds, if he doesn't tell us," said Bates.

"He'd know you wouldn't do it," said Bozzy.

"Who's game to go after him?" asked Jackson.

But there were no offers for this—the game wasn't worth the risk. Bates had been caught once before, and the interview with Dr. Blenkinsop that followed had left memories that were still painful. And there was plenty to do on the Moor. Indeed the time passed so quickly that, had it not been for Jackson—and one other—Billie might have made his return quite unobserved.

But at eight o'clock Jackson had his little army safely hidden in the bushes on each side of the gate, and ten minutes later he passed the word round that Billie was in sight. Five heads were craned out to watch. There came the truant—racing along the path with intent and serious air.

"Get ready," whispered Jackson. "The minute he's over the gate, on to him, and we'll have it out of him!"

"There won't be much time," said Simpson, who always saw the difficulties of any proposal first.

"What on earth——" broke in another voice, and the five watchers started and turned to find

Winthorpe Major staring at them. He had come up the grassy path quite unnoticed and unheard. " What on earth are you kids up to? "

One by one they crawled out and stood up sheepishly.

" What's the game? " demanded Winthorpe. " Don't you know it's just on roll-call? "

" We were just going to sprint off, Winthorpe," said Jackson.

" Do you usually do your sprinting lying down? " asked the school Captain. " Well, buzz off! Here—wait a minute "—as a thought came to him—" you weren't waiting for someone by any chance, were you? "

Now there was only one answer to this question that would have saved Billie, and that was an immediate " No." But even Jackson shrank from that, and Simpson even had the foolishness to look guiltily at the gate. Winthorpe swung round, and there, now but a few yards from the gate, was Billie.

The next minute his head appeared over the top as he swung himself up and then, and not till then, did he see the disaster that had befallen him. He stopped, one leg over the gate, staring at his brother, for once in his life stricken into silence.

"Come out of that!" said his brother curtly.

In dead silence Billie swung himself over and with an air of stolid nonchalance drifted up.

"You silly young ape!" said his brother. "What do you want to go out of bounds for?"

Billie only poked the turf with his toe. His brother looked at him searchingly and then turned to the five awed watchers.

"Buzz off, you!" he said angrily. "And if any of you are late, you'll do me fifty lines!"

They buzzed off, but not before Bozzy had made an effort to save their chum.

"We were only playing tracking, Winthorpe," he pleaded.

"Buzz off!" said Winthorpe.

And they had to go, leaving the irrepressible Billie a sad and sulky prisoner in the stern hands of Justice.

CHAPTER IV

A DESPERATE DEED

HAD anyone seen the tall, athletic Captain of the school and the chubby, cherubic junior walking side by side, he would never have guessed that they were brothers. Indeed an imaginative painter might have seen in them a suggestion for a new rendering of "Dignity and Impudence." There was nearly eight years difference in their ages, and Winthorpe Major at eighteen was a very serious young man indeed. He was proud of his position and took great pride in the reputation he enjoyed in it. His mischievous young brother, both at home and at school, had always been a thorn in his side. True, he had not thought it necessary to take any notice of him at school, but from time to time some reflection of his brother's troubles would fall upon him and make him squirm. Now he glanced at him savagely as he saw the hateful dilemma he was placed in.

It would be a grave neglect of his duty if he did not report this serious breach of rules to Dr. Blenkinsop. Yet, if he did, there would be silly sloppy talk about his high sense of honour, his strict impartiality, etc. He hated the thought of one as much as the other. He wanted the consciousness of doing right, but he hated the mere suspicion of acting like a prig. His ideal was the icily correct conduct that elicited neither praise nor blame.

"You young owl," he said angrily, "a pretty mess you've landed me in now, haven't you?"

Billie did not answer, but it seemed to him that it was he who was in a mess.

"What on earth did you want to go out of bounds for?"

"It—it was a game."

"Game! Isn't the Moor big enough for all the potty games you can play? The others didn't go out of bounds."

"No—they must have funked it," said Billie.

"Funked! That's you all over," cried his brother contemptuously. "You're the only kid in the school who isn't *afraid* to go out of bounds, I suppose? It doesn't occur to you, does it, that there are some kids in the school who like to play the game? What the Doctor will say to you I can't think."

Billie could only too well, and did not wish to dwell upon it. His brother, too, was very uneasy at the thought—it was just possible that the Doctor would suggest that he ought to keep a little closer watch on his brother, and try the effect of brotherly influence. The Doctor wasn't to know how utterly hopeless the elder brother knew that to be.

"Dick," said Billie, "need you tell the Doctor this once? Can't you——?"

"Is that your idea of being a sport?" asked his brother. "Let you off just because you're my brother? You little cad! Of course I must tell him."

"Dad will be awfully upset if I'm expelled," said Billie sadly.

"You won't be expelled," said his brother shortly. "It will be something much more painful than that."

"But isn't Blink—Dr. Blenkinsop away this week?"

"Yes, he is," said his brother, who had forgotten the fact. He thought for a minute. "I'll do just this much for you—as the Doctor is away, I'll report you to your house master and let him deal with you. I hope he thrashes you."

"Thanks," said Billie.

"You—you deserve it," said his brother, who was not without an uneasy feeling that he was acting rather like a bully.

When they reached the school roll-call was in progress, and the Captain, who was exempt from it, marched the delinquent straight to the master's study.

Mr. Bateson, the house master, was a portly, elderly man who dearly loved to spend his free evening hours alone with his pipe and his books. If there was one thing more than another he detested it was to have these pleasant interludes in a worrying life broken into by school business. It was therefore in a very snappish mood that he answered "Come in!" to Winthorpe's knock.

"You, Winthorpe?" he said in astonishment. "I'm very busy—won't it do some other time?"

"I'm afraid not, sir," said the Captain.

The master smothered an exclamation of impatience.

"Then come in," he said. "Who is that?" —as he caught sight of the form of the junior behind his brother. "Why, it's your brother, isn't it?"

"Yes, sir. I have brought him to you because I have just found him out of bounds—in the woods beyond the Moor."

"Out of bounds!" exclaimed the master.

"As Dr. Blenkinsop is away, sir, I thought I had better——"

"Quite, quite!" said Mr. Bateson. "You have only done your duty. What has he to say for himself?"

"Shall I leave you now, sir?" said Winthorpe Major.

"Yes, yes," said the master. "Now, Winthorpe, what have you been out of bounds for?"

That was a question that, Billie felt, permitted of no answer.

"Do you deny you have been out of bounds?"

"No, sir."

Mr. Bateson was a stern master; he was annoyed at being disturbed just now. He looked at Billie, but, in spite of his sternness and annoyance, he could not feel that righteous anger against him that the occasion called for. No one ever could. Deliberate disobedience to rules must be checked, but as he looked at the sturdy young rebel before him he knew only too well how difficult obedience must often be to that active, audacious mind. Indeed Billie at that moment was very nearly "getting away with it" again.

"You don't wish to tell me why you went out of bounds. Is that so?"

"Yes," said Billie. "I had a reason—I had to go—but I can't tell you why."

"But don't you see that if the reason was a good one, you would be able to tell me?" said Mr. Bateson. "This is a very serious offence. I must punish you very severely unless you can tell me something that might make it less serious. Why did you go?"

"There—there would have been a lot of suffering if I hadn't," muttered Billie.

"Suffering!" exclaimed Mr. Bateson. "By whom?"

Billie could only shake his head. Confession wouldn't save him. There was nothing he could tell Mr. Bateson that wouldn't make his offence ten times worse. He had been out of bounds, not once but half a dozen times, and then the prank he had been engaged in—it wouldn't be regarded as fun by a master. He couldn't "get away with it" this time, although he was aware the atmosphere was favourable.

"Very well," said Mr. Bateson. "As you will not speak, and may be meditating offending again at the first opportunity, you will be confined to the house till Dr. Blenkinsop returns. And, to prevent you being idle, you will write me out the first two hundred lines of the second book of the *Aeneid*. You may go."

Gated! As Billie made his way up to the dormitory, he was almost stunned by the disaster that had befallen him. A caning he had expected, or a heavy dose of lines, even a flogging by the Doctor—anything would have been preferable to being gated. For there was that in the woods which made it absolutely necessary that he should go at least once a day. It had only been a prank—now it was grim necessity. Go once more at least he must. How was it to be done?

Dormitory D were all on the alert when he entered.

"What did you get?" asked Jackie as Billie appeared.

"Gated!" said Billie, and went moodily to his bed.

"Gated! Is that all?" asked Bates, disappointed.

"All," said Billie. "No—two hundred lines of the *Aeneid*."

"You asked for it," said Bozzy.

"You don't know what it means," said Billie darkly. "You think it's only a joke. It isn't. It means—it means there'll be murder if I can't get out—that's what it means."

He started to fling off his clothes with such a desperate and defiant air that the chums looked at him in awe.

"Whom are you going to murder?" asked Jackson.

"I reckon *you've* asked for it," said Billie savagely. "The whole five of you—hanging about just where my brother could find you. If it hadn't been for you, he would never have seen me."

"How were we to know?" demanded Jackson.

"I'll tell you what," said Billie, as he got into bed. "You've got me into this hole—it's up to you to get me out of it."

"How d'you mean?" said Bates.

"I can't go into the woods now, can I?

Someone's got to go, and you'll have to take turns."

There was a moment's stupefied silence.

"What for?" said Jackson.

"I'll tell you before you go," replied Billie.

"Not me," said Bates. "I've done it before."

"Nor me," said Bozzy.

"I wouldn't mind doing some of the *Aeneid* for you, Billie," said Simpson timorously.

"You all funk it?" said Billie scornfully.

There was no time to reply as at that moment the corridor prefect entered, switched off the light, and commanded silence. But as Billie lay turning over in his mind the problem before him he knew that it was so—none of them would go. Besides, really he didn't want them to—if he could go himself. That was the problem—how?

The next day Billie passed in sulky silence. Being gated meant that he had to attend classes and the compulsory cricket in the afternoon as usual, but that in the free hours he had to report to the detention master.

His chums tried to show their sympathy in any little way they could, and Bates even smuggled a couple of doughnuts up into the dormitory for him, but he remained moodily silent.

The next day, on the playing fields, he managed to get Simpson to himself for a few minutes.

"Sim," he said, "you were always a sport, and you did offer to lend me a bob, didn't you?"

"Rather!" said Simpson eagerly. "Here—"

"No, I don't want it now," said Billie. "I want you to get something with it for me. Will you?"

"Of course," said Simpson.

"As soon as cricket's over, sprint off down to the village and get a good long rope—as much as you can for a bob. A clothes line will do if it's a strong one. Will you, Sim?"

"But—but why do you want a rope?"

"I'll tell you all about it to-morrow, Sim. But I must have it—to-day. Be a sport, Sim. You can easily get down to the village and back before tea and then run up to the dorm. and put the rope away in my locker."

"But—but——" hesitated Simpson.

"Do, old thing!" pleaded Billy. "If you don't, it will be so serious, Sim, you'll never forgive yourself—never!"

"All right," said Simpson reluctantly.

"Don't fail me, whatever you do," said Billy earnestly. "To-night—certain. It's a matter of life and death"—and with that he hurried back to his neglected position on the leg boundary.

Nothing more was said on the subject, but when Billie noticed at tea-time that Simpson came in very pink in the cheeks and with a furtive air of secret guilt, he knew that his request had been carried out. On going to the dormitory one glance at his locker showed him the rope—a hank of serviceable clothes-line which had cost the generous Simpson one-and-nine—and Billie gave his confederate a grateful wink. Nothing was said, however, and he got into bed in the sulky silence he had maintained for two days.

Apparently he was soon asleep, but Simpson could not get off. That rope was on his mind. What was Billie going to do with it? The dreadful thought had come to him that people hanged themselves with ropes. But Billie wasn't the sort for that. Yet—he was in sore disgrace, and "a matter of life and death," he had said. If he did, and it was his—Sim's—fault——

At last Sim fell asleep, but the dread haunted

him in his dreams. He saw figures hanging from trees, from windows, from gibbets—and always they were round, chubby figures of a boy about ten. Then he was out on the Moor. It was cold and dark, and he was running—running after someone, trying to stop him. He ran and ran, his breath came in panting gasps, but still the figure he was chasing kept just out of reach. Now he was in the woods—somehow he had got out of bounds without knowing it. He was in the glade down which Billie had come to his doom. He was running, running. Suddenly the glade ended in a wide clearing, in the centre of which was one small sapling. He stopped and watched it, for in his dream it seemed that this was what he had been chasing. And as he watched, the sapling began to grow—grow visibly before his eyes. Up, up it went, lengthening out like a gigantic scaffold pole—up far above the trees till the top was out of sight—like the beanstalk in the fairy tale.

Then from one of its topmost branches something began to descend, something wriggling and snakelike—a rope—a rope with a noose in the end of it—lower and lower it came—faster and faster—and then he could see that dangling in the noose was a ——

With a shriek of horror Simpson sat up in bed, wide awake, a cold sweat standing on his forehead.

"What's up?"

"Who's that?"

"What's the matter?"

The ejaculations came in sleepy tones from the startled sleepers as one by one they sat up. But Simpson had no eyes for them. He was staring at Billie's bed. It was empty. His horror-stricken gaze went to the window at the foot of the bed. The bottom sash was thrown right up. A full moon was riding high in the sky, and the dormitory was almost as light as day. To the iron bar that was fixed across the window frame a rope was secured, and it hung down outside. Simpson pointed to it in silent horror.

"Crumbs!" said Jackson, springing out of bed and going to the window. He had not had nightmare and therefore had no fears. He leaned out and pulled at the rope, which was quite slack.

"He's hooked it!" he said.

The other "Dormie D's" gathered round in awed silence. This was a desperate deed that simply staggered them—for a minute they could not think.

"He's mad," said Bozzy at last.

"Must be!" said Bates.

"Do you think he's run away?" asked Lucas.

"Do you think he's walking in his sleep?" ventured Simpson.

Meanwhile Jackson had been examining the rope. Knots had been made in it here and there, and it was just long enough to reach from the dormitory window on the second floor to the roof of a one-storey building that was used as the carpenter's shop. From this it was an easy drop to the ground.

"Sleep!" sniffed Jackson. "He's not asleep. He's gone off to the woods again—he said he must go."

"He's got some pluck," said Bozzy.

They stood looking at the rope, the garden, the playing fields and the Moor beyond—bathed in the silver radiance that makes its irresistible appeal to all human hearts, old and young alike—that appeal that makes the wisest of men at times play the fool. Their chum was out there in it somewhere—embarked on some desperate adventure—but already it no longer appeared so desperate as romantic and fascinating. Jackson, as usual, first put into words what they were all beginning to feel.

"I'll tell you what," he said. "He's got to be fetched back."

"But where's he gone?" asked Lucas.

"To the woods," said Jackson. "He's got some guilty secret. Who knows what may happen to him—all alone? We've got to go after him. Who's game?"

"He was always a decent kid," said Bozzy.

"But—but what if we're found out?" said Simpson.

"What if he dies out there—murdered? He said there'd be murder. It's our *duty* to go."

"We'd better take any grub we've got," said Bates.

"Besides," went on Jackson, "what would be said of us if we were found in bed when we knew our chum was out there alone? Blinkers would be pretty nasty about that!"

Although the entire conversation had had to be carried on in whispers, Jackson's determination carried the day. Besides, although all felt their action was a desperate one, there was something about the idea of sliding down that rope and tracking across the Moor in the glorious moonlight that had an impelling fascination, even over the timid Simpson.

In a few minutes they had scrambled into a few clothes and their gym. shoes. Two workable torches were found, but no grub. Jackson led the way, and one by one the boys slid down the rope. The descent was simplicity itself—a feat they had all frequently performed in the gym. They dropped from the low roof of the carpenter's shop into a bed of geraniums—that being expected to be the softest landing ground—and slunk silently across to the playing fields.

As they reached the gate a curious buffeting breeze sprang up—a kind of straggling wisp of cool air—and the next second a bank of black cloud swept over the moon, and the fields were suddenly plunged in inky blackness.

To the boys the sudden quenching of the moon seemed like the extinguishing of their beacon-light, and one or two of them felt the first tiny chill of fear. But Jackson was made of sterner stuff.

"That's lucky," he whispered. "No on
can see us now from the windows."

Across the fields they went at a trot, but ou
on the Moor beyond the way could only b
found by the aid of a torch. It was eerie ou
here among the gorse bushes in the blackness
and the wind was now rapidly rising. Th
bushes and trees groaned and creaked, and ther
were mysterious rustlings and buzzings all around
Lucas remembered that there were snakes or
the Moor, and stepped carefully, while Simpso
saw a thousand terrors in the unknown.

They reached the Dead Oak without misha
and in silence climbed the high railings of th
gate into the wood. Jackson was leading then
straight to the point where they had seen Billi
vanish on the former occasion, but so far there
had been no sign of him.

If it had been eerie on the Moor, it was ten
times more so in the woods. The wind tore
through the trees, tossing their branches about
with wild, unearthly noises, and every now and
again flinging a broken limb across their path.
Unseen creatures scuttled away from under their
feet, and once an owl hooted so suddenly within
a few yards of them that their hearts stood still.

Presently Jackson, going in front with a torch, stopped. There was a cross track running right and left, and he decided on the left. This rose steeply and after ten minutes or so brought them out of the wood on to the open hillside which was covered with brambles in which loose rocks and boulders were strewn. There could have been no more difficult country to cross in darkness, and the five chums floundered about, falling, slipping, stumbling, with very little idea in which direction they were going.

"How do you know we're going right, Jackie?" asked Bozzy.

"Where else can we go?" said Jackson. "He came down that track all right, because I saw his footsteps in the mud several times. Hallo! Rain!"

Big spots pattered down, and the lads stopped and peered around them. It seemed natural that their way should lay uphill, but that was about all the guidance Jackson had.

"All here?" he whispered.

"Yes," came the not very cheerful responses.

"We're here," said Bozzy, "but Billie isn't."

They struggled on for a few more minutes, and then suddenly a vivid flash of lightning lit up the whole hillside in front of them.

Just ahead of them was a clearing with some kind of rough shed at one side of it and above was the sharply defined ridge of the crest of the hill.

Then the thunder crashed overhead, and the rain suddenly changed from a soft patter to a deluge.

"Crumbs!" said Jackson. "Did you see that shed? Let's make for that."

They stumbled forward. Again the lightning flashed, and the thunder crashed, and the torrential rain drenched their scanty garments.

"Come on," said Jackson. "This way—here—we can sprint for it now"—and he was just about to do so when again the lightning lit up the hillside, and he stopped dead in his tracks, nearly paralysed by what the lightning had revealed.

For there was Billie. Billie without a doubt—clearly outlined on the ridge—Billie riding a ramping, galloping beast that was charging along with its head down and its heels kicking high behind.

It had been but an instantaneous glance, but it was unmistakable—Billie it was, although he looked as if he were posing as a ghostly centaur

-a fiend let loose by the storm and riding the
ind as though it were his native element.

They stood shivering in the dark and wet,
oo amazed even to speak, and before any of
hem had collected his thoughts or attempted
o move a terrific, nerve-racking bellow sounded
ust behind them. They leapt round, and at
hat instant again came the lightning glare, and
here, a yard or two from them, stood a bull,
awing the ground, with great horns curling
p from its lowered head.

In the weird blue light, and exaggerated no
oubt by their own jumpy nerves, it looked a
errifying object—a monster of most dreadful
nenace. Again it bellowed and tossed its head,
nd the group of lads in front of it scattered like
haff before the wind.

Simpson with a scream of terror fled towards
he woods. He heard again the fierce bellow,
he sound of trampling hoofs. Then he pitched
eadlong over a rock. He did not attempt to
ise, but partly crawling, partly rolling, he
loundered downhill till he came to the edge of
he wood and scrambled into the undergrowth.

Bruised, buffeted, torn, scratched, drenched,
nd panting, he struggled on, forcing his way

through the brambles and low growth. Tl storm was passing; the lightning was now le vivid, and the thunder was rumbling away int the distance. But the rain still came down i torrents, and the wind screamed among tl trees and tossed their boughs about in fury.

Somewhere in the wood, he felt, were h companions. He could see nothing, and t shout was hopeless, so great was the uproar c the tempest. Then suddenly he came out o to a grassy track where walking was easy. I ran downhill, and he felt it was leading towarc the school, and then the final catastrophe hap pened.

With a perfect tornado of sound, rending screeching, tearing, down came one of th giant elms with a crash that deafened Simpso and made the earth dance and quiver under him With a wild cry he turned and ran—only t put his foot deep in a hole and again to pitcl headlong in the darkness.

And the other fugitives in that wood—wher were they?

CHAPTER V

THE TRAGIC RETURN

THE full moon again rode in a serene sky. The heavy banks of cloud were now low on the horizon, their blackness still occasionally split by a lightning streak. Thunder was but a distant rumble, barely heard, and the wind that had raged so furiously had passed on with the storm clouds, leaving but a stray, wandering breeze to disturb the peaceful scene.

The window of Dormitory D was still thrown open to the night, and still from the iron bar hung the rope by which the "Dormie D's" had made their exit.

Two hours had passed, and now up the rope was struggling a bedraggled figure, panting hard as he hauled himself up. With an effort he swung himself over the sill and flopped down on the floor. And there he sat.

"Crumbs!" he muttered to himself. "Crumbs!"

His clothes were in an indescribable condition—torn, drenched, plastered with mud. His hair and hands and face were also covered in mud—apparently he had fallen into a bog. Streaks of blood showed in the ugly scratches on his face and hands.

"That's what comes of doing one's duty!" Jackson muttered bitterly, as he struggled to his feet. "Now what's to be done?"

He began taking off his soaked and muddy clothes, but even in this extremity he made an effort to avoid discovery. He rolled the shoes up in the knickers and jersey in a bundle that could possibly be concealed, using the jersey to wipe as much mud as possible from his hands and face, and had just got into his pyjamas, when he heard the sound of laboured breathing just outside the window.

He looked out, to see Bozzy hanging to the rope, at the last gasp. He stretched out and got hold of his clothing, and with this help Bozzy struggled over the sill. He was in an even more deplorable condition than Jackson.

"Wh—where are the others?" he stammered, as he gazed wild-eyed round the dormitory.

"Don't know," said Jackson.

"That awful crash—do you think it got any
 them?"

"Can't say," said Jackson. "Hope not. It
idn't get us."

The next to arrive was Bates. He seemed
esher and less damaged than the other two,
ut was even more sorry for himself. He lay
n the floor groaning.

"Shut up!" said Jackson. "Do you want
 wake the house? Get those things off and
et into bed."

"I'm absolutely starving," he whimpered, but
e saw the wisdom of obeying.

It seemed some time before Lucas appeared.
Ie was terribly distressed.

"Seen anything of Sim?" asked Bozzy.

Lucas shook his head.

"I wonder if that tree got him?" said
Bates.

"Or the bull?" said Jackson.

But no one had seen anything of him or of
ach other since the wild stampede that had
ollowed the sudden apparition of the bull. Each
ad ultimately found his way into the woods
nd so back to the Moor, missing by a miracle
he falling tree.

"Jackie, what are we going to do if he doesn turn up?" asked Bozzy.

But Jackson only shook his head. So far nc one word had been said of Billie. All had see that wild mounted figure, but none knew the others had, and, so fantastic had been th whole night's adventure, that no one was quit sure that the weird figure had really existec It was not till they were all sitting up in bec still anxiously waiting and watching for th missing Sim, that Bozzy put a tentative questior

"Did any of you see Billie?"

"I *thought* I did," said Lucas.

"So did I," said Bozzy. "In a flash o lightning. But he was *riding*."

"Yes, I saw him," said Jackson.

"So did I," said Bates. "On the top of th hill."

There was a silence, as each thought over thi amazing thing. What and why and how shoulc Billie be riding at midnight out in that wilc country? It beggared imagination.

"Bozzy, did you see *what* he was riding?" asked Lucas.

Bozzy shook his head.

"That's what beats me," he said. "It lookec

a huge creature—like one of those great bulls at the Zoo."

"It must have been a horse," said Jackson. "As if Billie could ride a bull!"

"Could he ride a horse for that matter, snorting and charging as if it were mad?" asked Bates.

"I'll tell you what," said Lucas in a solemn whisper. "It wasn't a horse—it was a monster—a unicorn or something—and Billie was bewitched!"

Jackson tried to laugh derisively, but to none of them did it seem the arrant nonsense it would have done at any other time.

Slowly the moon set. Still Simpson had not returned, but Dormitory D was now in darkness, and one by one the exhausted inmates slid down into their beds and slept.

Lucas was the first to wake. The others were still in the deep sleep of exhaustion, but Lucas, overwrought and overtired, had only had troubled and broken slumber. He sat up now with a jerk. It was morning, but for a minute Lucas could not get his bearings. He was oppressed with a sense of wild and terrible trouble hanging over him. What was it? Had the rising-bell gone? He glanced at his watch. Ten to seven. The bell wouldn't go for twenty-five minutes.

Then it all came back to him in a rush. Sim was not back, nor Billie, and the rope still hung from the open window. He looked out at the smiling countryside, glistening in the early sunshine, sweet and peaceful—for a minute he almost thought the whole adventure of the night had been a nightmare. Such wild and painful moments seemed to have no place in that land of blissful contentment. But then he felt the lump on the back of his head throb, and his bruises woke into smarting life one after the other, and he knew it had been no nightmare.

Panic seized him. What was to be done? Discovery seemed inevitable. He rushed to wake the others, but it was not easy. The first he attacked was Jackson. He shook and pummelled him, and when at last Jackie opened his eyes and saw Lucas bending over him, his first response was to aim a vicious blow at his face.

But Lucas hauled him out of bed, and by degrees Bozzy and Bates were prevailed upon to join them. It was a very serious Council of War that the four pyjamaed "Dormie D's" held by the open window. White-faced and heavy-eyed, scratched and bruised, with mud still to be seen on hands and heads, they met like the generals of a routed army—faced with surrender.

Billie's absence was his own concern—he had brought it on himself. But Simpson's—how could they account for that? If they denied all knowledge of it, would he not be sure to give them away? He might be injured—needing help—they couldn't leave him out there in the woods with a broken leg, perhaps, and pretend to know nothing about it. Yet what were they to do? Whom were they to tell?

In the cold light of morning their escapade looked so outrageous that the idea of going to Mr. Bateson and confessing it was appalling. It couldn't be done. Their hearts shrivelled at the thought of it. Nor could they face Matron. They could see her look of horror as they told her—her frenzied rush to Mr. Bateson—hammering on his door and bringing him out, in his most irritable mood, to come and hear this awful story—*that* couldn't be done.

Yet the minutes were passing. The rising-bell would go, and Matron would come bustling round. They looked at each other in gloomy despair. Then Jackson had an inspiration.

"I know," he cried. "Winthorpe Major. He's Captain, and he's Billie's brother—he ought to be told."

"That's it," said Bozzy.

"He may be so upset about Billie," said Bates, "that he may not ask any questions about *us*. We could tell the yarn artfully."

"How are we going to tell him?" asked Lucas. "All four of us go over to his house and tell him?"

"No, only one need go," said Jackson. "What about you, Lukey? He's fond of you."

"He's not!" said Lucas indignantly. "He hardly knows me. Besides, you ought to go, Jackie."

"You're the oldest," said Bates.

"And you can tell the best yarn," added Bozzy.

"No fear," said Jackson. "If you all funk it, there's only one thing to do—we must draw lots."

This finding favour, Jackson suggested the lot should be decided by seeing who could stand longest on the toes of the left foot with the right leg extended horizontally and held by the right hand, while the left hand was passed behind the head to grip the right ear. He happened to know that he was particularly good at keeping this trying pose.

The first to break down was Lucas—in less than a minute—and accepting his fate like a Stoic, he hurried into his clothes and departed sadly on his errand, a few minutes after the rising-bell had clanged through the house.

Winthorpe Major was in Hill House, and Lucas knew well the perils attaching to his embassy. He would be regarded by anyone who met him as an enemy within the camp, and he could not be sure that even the potentate to whom he was sent would respect his flag of truce.

However he reached Winthorpe's room without meeting anyone, and, feeling it was quite useless to knock on the door at that time of the morning, opened it and put his head within.

Winthorpe Major had just sat up in bed, and was still feeling the rebellious rage that the clang of the rising-bell rouses in most normal boys. He glared, stupefied, at the intruding head.

"Winthorpe," said a meek voice.

"Get out!" said the Captain.

"But, Winthorpe, I——" tried Lucas again coming into the room.

Winthorpe reached out his hand for the nearest missile, his slipper, and so Lucas blurted out his news before it arrived.

"Billie's missing."

Winthorpe arrested his hand and stared.

"What?"

"Billie's missing, and Simpson went to look for him and hasn't come back," explained Lucas.

Winthorpe looked at him incredulously for a minute and then sprang out of bed.

"Shut the door," he commanded sharply. "Now, tell me exactly what you mean."

So Lucas told him that Billie and Simpson were missing, and there was a rope hanging out of the dormitory window. He hoped that would be all he must tell. But he was mistaken.

Winthorpe was shocked. He had not an instant's doubt of what had happened. His reckless young brother in his disgrace had run away. It is only fair to him to say that his first feeling was anxiety for the young rebel, and the disaster he might have brought upon himself.

:ut quickly came the uneasy thought that per-aps he too was to blame—he had been harsh nd had never tried to help or guide the kid. Ie had always looked upon him as a nuisance ʼho would be sure to bring disgrace upon him. Vhat would Dad say? And the Doctor? And is fellow prefects? He squirmed as he saw ll the hateful fuss and talk that this would ıvolve.

But he quickly saw that immediate action of ome sort was necessary. Perhaps the young ɔol could be stopped and brought back before nyone heard of it. He began hurriedly to ress.

"When did you find out he had gone?" he sked sharply.

"When—when we woke," said Lucas.

"What time was that?"

"I—I don't know."

"Any idea where he's gone?"

"We think he went to the Moor."

"We? Who's we? How many know about t?"

"Only those in our Dormitory."

"Five of you?"

"Yes, but Simpson hasn't come back."

"Come back?" said Winthorpe.

"I mean he is missing too."

Winthorpe gave him a piercing glance.

"Get back to your dormitory—I'll be ove in a minute. All of you wait there for me."

Lucas went, but he had had no time to d more than announce the Captain's coming whe the great man himself was there.

The four juniors greeted him with deprecator grins and at once became absorbed in thei toilet. Winthorpe looked at them—at thei white, scratched faces and lack-lustre eyes. H went to the window and looked at the rope. H looked at the window sill and then at the floo below it. He turned to the juniors, but no one was facing him.

"You say my brother and Simpson got ou of this window?"

"Yes, Winthorpe," came in a chorus.

"And haven't come back?"

"No, Winthorpe."

"Then who did come back? Look at th mud on the sill! Look at the floor! A whol crowd of you have been out and back again.' He seized Lucas, who happened to be nearest by the collar and shook him angrily. "Yo

oung liars! You know all about it. Tell me
ll you know this minute!"

"We woke up and found Billie gone, and we
–we went to find him," stammered Lucas.

"We thought we ought," put in Jackson.
He—he might have been hurt."

"What time was that?"

"We don't know."

"Was it light?"

"The moon was shining."

"Did you find him?"

"We saw him. He was up on the hill through
he woods, and he was riding."

"Riding?" said Winthorpe. "What?"

"We don't know," said Lucas. "It was huge
nd wild and galloping."

"We only saw him in a flash of lightning,"
xplained Jackson.

Bit by bit Winthorpe got out of them all they
ould tell. His first feeling was relief. Wild
nd improbable as this tale was, it was clear
Billie had not run away—it was not he who had
driven him to this desperate deed. How much
o believe and what to make of it he did not
know, but he saw at once it was too serious a
matter for him to deal with.

"You get dressed and stay here till I com back," he said curtly, and went off to M Bateson's room.

Ten minutes elapsed, and the Captain returne with the house master. Mr. Bateson was n angry—he was too appalled. Six of his boy out in the dead of night—it was a state of thing he could not bring himself to believe in.

The questioning began all over again, an the poor "Dormie D's" squirmed on the rac once more.

"There is only one thing to be done, sir, said the Captain at last. "If you will allow m to take out a search party—I know that hu the boys describe on the hillside. We could g there and search the woods. They may hav met with an accident."

"I must 'phone the police, and the Doctor,' said Mr. Bateson. "I cannot take the respon sibility."

"If you give me an hour first, sir, perhap it won't be necessary."

"Very well. Go by all means. You may tak any of the prefects, and the gardener and boo boy, and—and anyone else. But I must certainly 'phone the police."

"*Look!*"

The exclamation came from Jackson, and he was pointing out of the window and staring goggle-eyed. Master, Captain, and boys all swung round and looked, and all gave vent to exclamations of astonishment, staring too.

There, coming across the playing fields, was Winthorpe Minor, leading a donkey with one hand and with the other holding Simpson on the donkey's back. Billie's face was the colour of chalk; he limped wearily; he was obviously on the verge of complete exhaustion. Simpson was in even worse plight. His face was drawn with pain; and he clutched desperately at the donkey's neck and seemed all but unconscious. It was a tragic return.

Winthorpe Major was the first to recover from his astonishment. With an exclamation he dashed from the room.

With one accord the "Dormie D's" turned to follow him, but Mr. Bateson blocked the way.

"Stop!" he said sternly. "You will stay here, all of you, till Matron has seen you. Jackson, untie that rope and shut the window."

He went out, and they saw Winthorpe Major meet the culprits on the playing fields. They saw Billie grin up at his brother, and say something which they couldn't hear, and then pitch forward on his face.

Mr. Bateson came out then, and Matron. There was running to and fro. The ambulance was brought, and first one and then the other of the returned fugitives were carried over to the San.

They heard the breakfast bell go, and the boys trooping down, all unaware of anything unusual. Still they waited. They were in no mood for disobedience, and those still forms, with the death-like faces, being carried in had struck awe into their hearts. They sat in silent misery, waiting.

At last Matron came. But she would answer no questions. She knew what they had been through and saw they were not far from exhaustion. Dormitory D was turned into a hospital ward. All four were ordered to bath and get back to bed, their bruises and scratches were examined and treated, their muddy clothes were removed, medicine was administered to prevent chill, and bread and milk provided for breakfast.

Then the blinds were drawn down, and they were bidden to sleep.

"But, Matron," said Lucas pleadingly, "Simpson is not dead, is he?"

"No, he is not dead," said Matron. "But he has a broken ankle. Now go to sleep, all of you."

But sleep seemed the last thing possible. However, tired as they were after their wild night, one by one they dropped off, and it was afternoon before any of them woke.

CHAPTER VI

BILLIE EXPLAINS

THE "Dormie D's" did not wake to an
very pleasant thoughts. They were sor
and stiff and hungry, but worst of all the
knew that the near future could hold nothin
very pleasant for them. Their offence was rank
and punishment must be dire. Would they b
expelled? Sent home as unfit for Harleyford
They all squirmed at the thought of facing thei
home people with this indelible mark of disgrac
upon them. Everyone would know. They
would be pointed out as the bad boys of th
neighbourhood—perhaps sent to some potty littl
day school, or one of those institutions wher
boys not fit for decent schools were taken.

Too dejected even for speech, they lay and
waited till Matron came in. She took their
temperatures and examined their hurts, and as
none seemed now much the worse for their
night's adventure, she bade them all get up and

go into Form III Common Room, where tea would be brought them.

As they had had no dinner, eggs were provided, and as this was the first square meal they had had for nearly twenty-four hours, they did full justice to it, and at once began to feel more cheerful.

Their rising spirits were immediately dashed, however, by a summons to Mr. Bateson's room. But the result was only a prolongation of their suspense, for the house master had decided the matter must be left for Dr. Blenkinsop to deal with. Meanwhile they were to be confined to their dormitory and Common Room. They would see no other boys; meals would be brought to them; and they would occupy themselves with construing and writing out one hundred lines of the second book of the *Aeneid*.

"And if I hear the slightest noise from you," he concluded, "or there is the least suspicion of disorderly conduct, I shall deal very severely with you. As it is, your punishment will be severe. I advise you to do nothing to add to it."

The warning was not necessary. For the present the spirit of the "Dormie D's" was broken.

A very miserable three days passed. Not th least trying part of their ordeal was their isolatio from the school, and their consequent ignoranc of what was happening. Matron had told then that Simpson's ankle was not broken after all— only very badly sprained, and he was doing well but that was all she would say. They still dic not know what mad prank it was that Billi had been playing, what he was doing on tha wild night, and how he had found Sim. They could imagine all the wild surmise and rumou that was flying through the school. And here they were—the parties most vitally concerned— shut out of it all, and driven to asking each other the same old questions which nobody could answer.

On Monday morning they were summoned to the Doctor's study. He had returned on Saturday. He was seated at his desk in his gown in an attitude that seemed to give him a judicial status. The pale and spiritless quartette that was formed up in line before him would not have thought it very incongruous had he worn a wig and the black cap. Neither Billie nor Simpson was present, but Winthorpe Major was there with a grave-looking gentleman whom ey all guessed at once to be Billie's father. heir hearts sank even lower. Was it to be xpulsion?

The proceedings, however, were brief. The octor sternly told them of what they were ccused—" breaking out of the school at night a manner almost too outrageous to be believed" -and asked if anyone had any explanation to ffer.

Jackson had intended to explain that they nly did it because they thought it was their uty to see Billie came to no harm, but he ouldn't get it out—it didn't seem as though it ould hold water, somehow—and they were all lent.

"This is the most serious offence I have ever nown committed by boys of your age," said ne Doctor sadly, "and I should be quite ıstified in expelling you—quite. However, om what I have been told I am willing to believe ıat you were actuated by some ridiculous idea ıat you were going to the aid of a companion ho was in trouble, and I will take that into ccount. You must all know perfectly well that our first duty on finding your companion missing as to go to the corridor prefect or the house

master, so that proper help could be obtaine
You know also that rules and bounds *must* b
kept. To help to impress it upon you, you wi
all be confined to your house and your pock
money will be stopped till the end of the tern
You may go."

Crushed by the stern tone and icy aloofne
of the Doctor, the four "Dormie D's" wer
escorted back to their Common Room.

Gated for the rest of the term. It was prett
awful, but they all felt it might have bee
worse.

"Anyway, there'll be cricket," said Bozzy.

"No pocket money means no tuck," sai
Bates dismally.

"Do you good," said Jackson. "You're fa
enough. But I wonder what's going to happe
to Billie. Did you see his old man was there?

"Looks like expulsion," said Bozzy.

"Poor old Billie!" said Lucas. "We shal
miss him."

"He *was* a lively kid," said Jackson. "An
he had pluck."

"But, if he's sent off right away, we shal
never know what he's been up to," said Bozzy

"He may write," said Jackson.

However Billie was not expelled, and later that evening, to the delight of the "Dormie D's," he suddenly joined them in the Common Room.

"Hallo, kids!" he said, with his familiar grin, but that deceived no one. The grin was too obviously not of the kind that wouldn't come off, and they knew he had suffered.

"What have you got?" asked Jackson.

"Gated and no pocket money till the end of term," said Billie.

"Same as us," said Jackson.

"Blinkers was going to expel me, but my Dad talked him over, and old Dick—I must say he turned up trumps. Said he was sure it was only high spirits and he would look after me if I had another chance. Can you see him doing it? My, there'll be some fun!"

"But what did you do with the donkey and where did you get it?" asked Bozzy.

"Where did you find Sim?" asked Bates.

"You ought to tell us all about it now, Billie," said Lucas reproachfully.

So Billie did. Seated on the table, with the others gathered around him, hanging on every word, he told his tale.

"You remember that last Nature walk we had with old Bateson and the donkey we saw? And how wild Bateson was because we tried to ride it? Well, I didn't say anything, but I went off a few days afterwards to see if I could get a ride on the quiet, but it was in the farmyard then, and the old farmer was there.

"He was a decent sort though, and chatty, and I asked him how much a donkey like that would cost. He said he didn't know, but that one wasn't much good to him, and he'd sell it for a pound or so."

"Oh! That's what you did with the pound note!"

"Yes. It came the very next week, on the Monday, and I went straight off. It looked as though it had been sent on purpose—just when I wanted it, and I couldn't let the chance go. The farmer seemed a bit suspicious at first—said he had been joking—but I showed him the pound note and said I could take the donkey away with me to a good home, and he let me have it.

"I couldn't bring it to the school, could I? I had to hide it somewhere. I meant to find a place in the woods, near the Moor, where we ould hop over easily and have no end of fun, ut then I remembered that old shed out on ıe hillside, and that seemed just the place. No ne ever went there, and the donkey would be ıeltered and hidden, and I could get to it every ay to feed it and take it to drink.

"That was the trouble. I tied it up all right ı the shed—the farmer had given me a rope alter, but no saddle—and I gave it plenty of rass and stuff to eat, but I had to take it over he top of the hill to a pond to drink. It was un, I can tell you, riding it over, and it was o frolicsome."

"But why didn't you tell us?" asked Bozzy.

"I was going to," said Billie, "as soon as I ould get it nearer. And I wanted to, but I aw it wouldn't do. It was risky enough my oing out of bounds every day. If all the six f you had gone, and you know you would ıave done, the game would have been up at nce. Then you began to get nosey about it, nd what I had done with the pound note, and hat made it all the more fun. It was such a ine rag, I *couldn't* tell you. Besides, I couldn't ide much at first—ever tried galloping bare ack?—and I wanted to be able to do a few

tricks before I let you in. I used to think wha
a grand rag I'd have—on breaking-up day per
haps—riding to the station on my own mok
and doing tricks all the way. How you woul
have gaped!"

"But what happened in the storm?" sai
Bozzy. "We saw you."

"I know—Sim told me in the San.," sai
Billie, with a sidelong look. "When I wa
gated, you can see the fix I was in. The donke
was tied up, no one knew where, and if I couldn'
get out, it would die of thirst. I stuck it fo
two days, and then—well, I had to go, hadn'
I? Sim got the rope for me, and it was al
quite easy till the storm came. I had taken th
moke over to drink, and it caught us on top o
the hill. Poor old moke, it was terrified. I
galloped about, and kicked, and snorted—you
might have thought it was a mad bull."

"We did," said Bates.

"So Sim said."

"But it couldn't have been a donkey you were
riding—it looked huge," objected Bozzy.

"It was," said Billie. "It must have been the
lightning magnified it. It does, you know. And
the moke was fierce that night. I don't suppose

it did look like a donkey. It threw me off—that's how I got so knocked about, and I chased all over the hillside for miles looking for it before I thought of going to the shed—and there it was, standing there quietly munching. I believe it'd gone straight back. I tell you, I felt the ass, not it.

"I tied it up, and started home, but it was hard getting through the wood because of the fallen tree. Then I came on Sim—heard him moaning. I tried to get him up, but he couldn't stand—said he had broken his leg. I sat by him for a time, then tried to carry him on my back, but I was too done up. He told me you had all come out, and I didn't know what to do—if I came up to the school for help it must give you away, and I thought perhaps you were all safe. Suddenly I thought of the moke, and saw it was just the thing.

"It was light then, so I went back and fetched it. It was a bit of a job getting it through the woods, and Sim didn't seem as though he could keep on, and then I had to make a hole in the hedge—you can tell I was a bit done when I got here."

"You looked it," said Jackie.

"What's happened to the donkey?" asked Lucas.

"The gardener's looking after it, and Dad said he would dispose of it," said Billie sadly. "It couldn't be helped, of course—I had to do it for poor old Sim—but the fun's over now."

"Over! I should say it jolly well is," said Bozzy.

"You talk of fun," said Jackson bitterly. "It's you who've had the fun, we haven't, and we've got to suffer for it."

"That's your own silly fault," said Billie.

"Why is it?" snapped Jackson.

"'Course it is," said Billie. "It was decent of you to come to look for me, but if you hadn't been such mugs I should never have been caught!"

"Oh!" said Jackson, but that was all he could say. It was possible that Billie would "have got away with it," as he always did.

PRINTED FOR THE PUBLISHERS BY PURNELL AND SONS, PAULTON (SOMERSET) AND LONDON